This is a book about **CAKE**, all different types of cake. If you like to **EAT** cake or **BAKE** cake, then this is the book for you.

Warning—this book may make you **HUNGRY** . . .

For my agent
Catherine Pellegrino

Illustrated by
Dave Shephard, based on
original illustrations by
Alex G. Griffiths

First American Edition 2021
Kane Miller, A Division of EDC Publishing

Copyright © Harriet Whitehorn and
Oxford University Press 2021
Illustrations © Alex G. Griffiths 2021
Freddie's Amazing Bakery: The Sticky Cake Race was originally
published in English in 2021. This edition is published by
arrangement with Oxford University Press.

For information contact:
Kane Miller, A Division of EDC Publishing
5402 S 122nd E Ave, Tulsa, OK 74146
www.kanemiller.com
www.usbornebooksandmore.com

Library of Congress Control Number: 2020936315

Printed and bound in the USA
1 2 3 4 5 6 7 8 9 10

ISBN: 978-1-68464-069-0

FREDDIE'S
AMAZING BAKERY

THE STICKY CAKE RACE

WRITTEN BY
**HARRIET
WHITEHORN**

ILLUSTRATED BY
**ALEX G.
GRIFFITHS**

Kane Miller
A DIVISION OF EDC PUBLISHING

Our story is set in a town called *Belville* —look, here is a map of it. As you can see, it is a delightful place, just the right size, and crisscrossed by a spiderweb of pretty canals (perfect for boating in the summer and skating in the winter), which are lined with cherry trees and tall old houses.

MAGNOLIA CANAL

BELVILLE THEATRE

BELVILLE MUSEUM

CHAPTER ONE

It was a warm, sunny day, right at the beginning of September, and there was a back-to-school feeling in Belville. The long, lazy days of the summer were over, and everyone, however old they were, felt like they should be polishing their shoes and organizing their pencil cases.

Freddie, boy baker, owner of Freddie's Amazing Bakery, and our hero, was cycling around the town with his dog, Flapjack. Can you see

Flapjack sitting in the basket on the front of Freddie's bicycle? They were on the way to Van de Lune's Hotel with a very special delivery when Freddie saw a familiar figure, walking along the street.

Flapjack gave a friendly bark, and Freddie called, "Hi, Noah!" Noah ran the café in the park, and he was one of Freddie's best friends and his kung fu partner. He was carrying a pail of glue and a brush and had a large bag slung over his shoulder.

"Are you putting up posters for the Belville Charity Rally?" Freddie asked excitedly.

"I most certainly am," Noah replied. "It's only a couple of weeks away now." He fished a poster out of his bag and opened it up to show Freddie. "Isn't this **beautiful?** Jojo designed it for me,"

Belville
CHARITY RALLY

◆

1st PRIZE
A brand-new roadster bike

BEST COSTUME PRIZE
A showstopper cake made by Freddie's Amazing Bakery

£10 ENTRANCE FEE FOR CHARITY

Noah said. Jojo was a friend of theirs.

"Fantastic!" Freddie cried.

"And look what Ralph at the cycle shop gave me," said Noah, pointing to the poster. "A brand-new roadster bike for the winner!"

"Wow! That's so generous!" Freddie exclaimed.

"Thanks again for offering to make a cake for the best costume prize," Noah said. "The one you made last year was amazing."

"Well, I'm not sure about that," Freddie said modestly. "But I'm really looking forward to making it. By the way, is the race along the same route as last year?"

Noah shook his head. "No, not after the CRASH on Green Canal last year. No one was actually hurt, but the mayor is worried that someone might be if it happens again, so we're going along Main Canal instead. Do you want to help me at the finish line again this year?" Noah asked.

"I'm afraid I can't. I'm taking part!" Freddie said. "I'm so excited! Sophie, you know, my assistant at the bakery, is a super-keen cyclist, and she and Amira have been getting really excited about the race. A couple of weeks ago they bought an old three-seater bicycle from a junk shop. Sophie has been tinkering around with it ever since."

"A three-seater bicycle! That's so cool. What do you call one of those?"

"I don't think they have an official name, but we've been calling it the tridem!"

Noah laughed. "A tridem! Like a

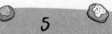

tandem but for three! I love that. And what about Flapjack?"

"There's a basket on the front for him, of course!" Freddie said. "We wouldn't want to leave you out, would we?" He stroked Flapjack's head.

Noah laughed and was about to say goodbye when he noticed the huge box on the back of Freddie's bike.

"Wow! What have you got in there?" he asked.

"A wedding cake," Freddie replied. "I'm taking it over to Van de Lune's Hotel, where the wedding reception is tonight. It's one of the first I've made, and I think it looks OK, but I'm a bit nervous about it."

"Ooh, can I see it?" Noah asked.

"Sure," Freddie replied. And he propped his bike up, hopped off, and

opened the box to reveal an amazing cake.

"The couple getting married wanted a traditional tiered wedding cake, but with a boating theme—they're very keen sailors."

"Freddie, it's fantastic! They are absolutely going to love it!"

"I hope so," Freddie said nervously.

"Now, I'd better get these posters up. Do you mind sticking one in the bakery window?" Noah asked.

"Of course not," Freddie said.

"Thank you," said Noah, and he handed him a rolled-up poster. "See you at kung fu later!"

"See you later," Freddie replied, and he cycled off with Flapjack.

Freddie delivered the wedding cake and then headed back to the bakery.

"Hi, Sophie. Look what I've got!" Freddie announced as he walked into the kitchen. Sophie was busy making a batch of sausage rolls. Flapjack (who was very fond of sausage rolls) bounded over to her hopefully.

Freddie noticed that Sophie looked upset, so before she could reply he asked, "Is everything OK?"

"Someone stole my bike last night, from outside my house," she said with a sigh.

"Not the tridem?" Freddie asked.

"No, my normal bike that I use to cycle here," she said.

"Poor Sophie had to take three different buses to get to work this morning," Amira said, coming into the kitchen. Amira was another of Freddie's best friends, and she managed the bakery for him.

"Oh, I'm so sorry," Freddie said. "Maybe this will cheer you up." He showed Sophie the race poster. "And look, the prize is a bike."

Sophie looked at it.

"That's a fantastic bike," she said.

"Well, we'll just have to make sure that we win it for you," Amira announced. "We'd better make some decisions very soon about our costumes and decorating the tridem."

"I've got so many ideas!" Sophie replied, gesturing to the kitchen wall where she'd been pinning up sketches of different costumes.

Their race talk was interrupted when a voice called "Amira!" from the shop.

"I'd better get back to the customers, but shall we all have a chat after work?" Amira suggested.

"I'm at kung fu practice," Freddie said. "But I'm happy with whatever you two decide."

"You might regret that," Sophie joked.

"I trust you!" Freddie replied with a laugh. "Now, Sophie, shall we go through the orders for tomorrow?" Sophie agreed, and they got to work.

CHAPTER TWO

Over on Main Canal, a middle-aged man and a large tabby cat were sitting in the sun outside a shop called Macaroon's Patisserie. The cat's name was Otto, and his owner was a baker called Bernard Macaroon. While Bernard was sunning himself, he was also reading a book called *How to Win at Everything*

by Drusilla Green and was so absorbed that he hardly noticed when Noah walked up to him.

"Hi, Bernard, how are you?" Noah asked.

"Busy," Bernard replied rudely, without looking up from his book. Otto gave Noah an evil look.

Noah decided not to be put off, and went on, "Would you mind putting a poster in the patisserie window? It's for the Charity Rally," he explained.

The words "Charity Rally" caught Bernard like a fish on a hook. The race was one of his favorite things in the whole world.

"Of course not!" he cried, suddenly all smiles. "I was just thinking about the race." And, when Noah looked puzzled, he held up his book so that Noah could read the title. "You must remember that I should have won last year," Bernard went on. "I was robbed of the title due to that business on Green Canal."

"Oh yes, I'd forgotten that it was you who . . ." Noah stopped himself from saying "caused the crash" as he thought it sounded too rude. "That you were involved."

"As always, I bore the brunt of everyone else's mistakes," Bernard said with a long sigh.

That was not how Noah remembered it, but he decided it was best to say nothing except, "All the race details are on the poster." He pulled one out of his bag and handed it to Bernard. "Thank you."

"My pleasure," Bernard replied, practically snatching the poster from

Noah. Bernard had no intention of putting it anywhere—the fewer people who entered the race the better, as far as he was concerned. But he wanted to have a good look at the poster himself, so as Noah walked off, he unrolled it. "Ten pounds entrance fee for charity!" he tutted. "What a ridiculous waste of money! And drat, it's still a costume ride!" Bernard considered dressing up beneath his dignity.

But then he saw the prizes.

That's a very expensive-looking bike, he thought, admiring the picture.

He imagined himself riding around Belville on it, and everyone saying, "Goodness me, Bernard must be very rich to afford such a bicycle."

Smiling at the thought, he looked at the rest of the poster.

"Best costume prize, a showstopper cake from Freddie's Amazing Bakery," he read. "Yuck! We don't want to win that, do we, Otto?"

Bernard secretly loved Freddie's cakes because how could you not when they were so delicious? But he was also very jealous of Freddie and his talent, so he would never admit it.

"I suppose we could have some fun squashing Freddie's horrible cake over his smug head," Bernard chortled.

Otto gave a sort of bad-tempered meow in response.

"Right, Otto, let's work out how we are going to win," said Bernard, picking up his book again.

Never had Bernard enjoyed a book so much, and he thought of its author, Drusilla Green, as his new best friend. A particularly nice best friend who told him everything he liked to hear in short, snappy sentences such as, "Winning is a natural desire—own it." And, "You're worth it. Lots of people don't win things because deep down they don't think they're worth it, but YOU ARE."

Drusilla had written two hundred and fifty pages about winning, but it really boiled down to her Six Golden Rules:

Rule Number 1 *Think Positively.*
Tell yourself that you are brilliant, and you will be.

Well that's easy enough, Bernard thought, *because I am brilliant.*

Rule Number 2 *Dress for Success.*
It was actually Bernard's costume that had caused the trouble on Green Canal the previous year. He had dressed up as a knight in armor (which Bernard felt was suitably heroic), but the visor on his helmet kept slipping down so he couldn't see anything. And when this happened on Green Canal, he was going so fast that he skidded all over

the road, crashing into people and causing the crash. So, although Bernard wouldn't admit that it was his fault, he did make a mental note that he must choose a costume that was practical.

Rule Number 3 *Be Prepared.*
Bernard remembered that his bicycle was in the corner of his garage with a flat tire, so he'd better get that fixed. He glanced down at his tummy. Perhaps he should do a few sit-ups too, and generally do a bit more exercise and eat less cake.

Rule Number 4 *Learn from Your Mistakes.*
Apart from his costume issues, Bernard considered his main mistake the previous year to be not cheating enough. Bernard adored cheating, and he never felt bad about it. And so he particularly loved Drusilla's Rule Number 5 . . .

Rule Number 5 *Do Whatever You Need to do to Win.* (A little helping hand is OK. Use whatever it takes to give you extra confidence.)

Bernard smiled to himself—there was nothing he loved more than a "helping hand" or, as others might call it, cheating.

Now, there was a Rule Number 6, but Bernard always ignored it because it was one bit of Drusilla's advice that he didn't agree with. But I will tell it to you anyway. It was . . .

Rule Number 6 *Sometimes Even Winners Lose.* And when they do, they are good losers because that way they are really winners.

Nonsense! Bernard thought, when he read it. *A loser is a loser!*

CHAPTER THREE

Over the following days, excitement about the race rippled through the streets of Belville, and in every home, office, café, and shop, people chatted about it nonstop —who would take part, what they would wear, and who was likely to win. And at Freddie's Amazing Bakery, it was just the same.

"So, tell me, Amira, are you entering the race this year?" Dr. Wells, the vet, asked, as Amira packed up a box of lemon tarts for him.

"I am indeed," she replied. "Along with Sophie and Freddie. And what about you?"

"Absolutely. I was up half the night sewing my costume," Dr. Wells said, stifling a yawn.

At that moment, the shop telephone rang. Sophie and Freddie were busy in the kitchen, so Amira said, "Sorry, I'd better answer that—I'll be as quick as I can," and she went over to the phone and picked up the receiver. "Freddie's Amazing Bakery. Amira speaking."

"Hello, Amira, it's Harry from the hardware store here."

He sounds stressed, Amira thought, so she replied, "Hi, Harry, are you OK?"

"I've had a bit of a disaster," Harry replied. "It's my daughter Lily's birthday today, and I've totally forgotten to buy a cake. I can't leave the shop at the moment, and she'll be back from school in about an hour—she's going to be really upset, so I just wondered if there was any way that someone could bring something over? I'm very sorry to ask because I know you're always busy."

"Don't worry. We'll sort something out," Amira said. "Is there anything she particularly likes?"

"She loves chocolate," said Harry.

"Great. I'll just go and talk to Freddie, and one of us will bring something around to you soon."

"Thank you so much, Amira, you've saved my life," Harry said gratefully.

Amira finished packing up the lemon tarts for Dr. Wells and then went into the kitchen and explained about Harry to Freddie.

"Poor Harry!" Freddie said. "He must be in such a panic." And then he paused, looking around the kitchen. "But there's no time to make anything, and I haven't got any chocolate cakes left."

"How about brownies?" Sophie suggested. "There's a big batch that's ready to come out of the oven."

"Perfect," Freddie replied. He took the brownies out and, after he'd let them cool for a few minutes, he cut them into eighteen squares and piped *HAPPY BIRTHDAY LILY!* across them in thick gold icing.

Then he put them in a box, along with some candles in case Harry didn't have any.

"I'll take them to Harry's. I could do with some fresh air," Freddie announced. He hopped on his bike with Flapjack and whizzed off.

Freddie was just drawing up outside Harry's shop—Harry's House of Hardware—when he felt himself ride over something in the road. His front wheel made a noise somewhere between a **BANG** and a **CLUNK**, and there was a **HISSING** sound as all the air rushed out of the tire.

Oh rats! Freddie thought. He hopped off his bike and looked. There was a small cardboard box on the road labeled

TACKS, and several large tacks (which are like a cross between a nail and a thumbtack) were stuck in his tire.

The tire was as flat as a pancake.
"How annoying!" Freddie said to

Flapjack. "Someone must have bought the box at Harry's and then dropped it." He sighed and then said, "Oh well! Worse things happen. Best get the brownies in to Harry before Lily comes back from school." He lifted Flapjack out of the basket, and then together they took the brownies inside the shop.

Harry was delighted to see them. "Freddie, you're a lifesaver!" he exclaimed, peeking into the box. "Fantastic! Thank you so much. Let me pay you," he said, opening the till and getting some money out.

"Thanks, Harry," Freddie said as he took the money from him.

"Is there anything I can do for you?" Harry asked.

"Actually, there is something. Someone dropped a box of tacks outside your shop, and they've punctured my front wheel. Do you have a tire repair kit?"

"Oh no, what a pain! I do have a kit—I'll just get it and if you bring the bike in here, I'll help you."

Across town at Macaroon's Patisserie, Bernard was about to go into his office and pretend to do some work (but probably have a snooze), when he decided he was a bit hungry. So, he walked into the kitchen. All the patisserie staff were talking excitedly about the rally.

"Hi, Bernard," said Tom, who worked in the kitchen. "We've just decided to enter the race as a team from the patisserie."

28

Bernard frowned. "What on earth is the point in that?" he asked. "There's only one prize, and you can't share it."

"Oh, we're just doing it for fun, and to raise money for the charity. We're not really bothered about winning," Tom replied.

"Not bothered about winning?" Bernard spluttered. "How extraordinary!"

"So, you don't want to be part of the team?" Tom asked quickly.

As you can imagine, Bernard was not the most popular boss, so everyone waited nervously for him to reply. They let out a silent sigh of relief when he said, "Certainly not. I don't want to be involved with a bunch of losers! Now you lot, get back to work," he went on. "And Tom? Where are this morning's croissants? I need to have one to check that you haven't messed them up."

CHAPTER FOUR

Once he'd gotten himself a croissant (and a *pain au chocolat*, and a *pain au raisin*, just to be sure), Bernard went back to his office. He sat down at his desk and looked at his To Do list for the race.

TO DO
1 Outfit
2 Bicycle
3 Diet and exercise
4 "Helping hands"

The day before, Bernard had been to Tippy Top Tailors to order his costume. After a lot of consideration, he had decided to keep it simple and to the point, and to dress up as a king. As usual, Tippy Top had been very helpful and suggested a magnificent (but snug-fitting) crown, and a glittery gold outfit, with a matching outfit for Otto. *Very good,* Bernard thought, putting a big check next to number 1.

Number 2 on the list was bicycle, and later that day he was going to take his bicycle over to Dodgy Dave's Bike Shop to have the puncture mended and the bike painted gold to match his outfit. *Another check for that,* Bernard thought, feeling pleased with himself.

Next on the list was diet and exercise. He took a big bite of *pain au chocolat* as he thought about this. Bernard had to admit that it hadn't gone so well recently—basically apart from a bit of strolling around Belville, Bernard had done zero exercise and eaten just as many cakes, pastries, and biscuits as normal.

I'll start that tomorrow, he decided and quickly moved on to the more cheerful subject of "helping hands," or cheating.

Bernard had worked out that in a race such as the Belville Rally there were two forms of cheating:

- Things that made it easier for him to win.

- Things that made it more difficult for everyone else to win.

But unusually for Bernard, he didn't have any specific ideas. He sat at his desk, fidgeting, ho-ing, and hum-ming, but nothing came to mind.

I am lacking inspiration, he thought, and he decided to consult his book. He looked up "inspiration" in the index at the back, and it told him to turn to page 234, so he did:

"I find inspiration often strikes in the strangest times," Drusilla had written. "I always get my best ideas in the shower! Or, strangely, when something bad happens, it can really inspire me—remember the old saying: when life gives you lemons, make lemonade! But if you're totally stuck, my advice is to get out from behind your desk and take a brisk walk. It always gets the creative juices flowing!"

Right, a brisk walk then, Bernard thought. He made his way out through the kitchen toward the back door, but, unfortunately, he failed to notice a large pool of golden syrup on the floor. He walked straight through it, his suede loafers sticking to the floor like glue.

"FOR GOODNESS' SAKE!!" he shouted. The room was empty, but a second later, Tom came back in clutching a mop and bucket full of hot, soapy water. His face fell when he saw Bernard.

"Oh, Bernard! I'm SO sorry. The tin was really slippery, and then the lid came off."

"I don't want to hear your excuses!" Bernard ranted at him. "Last week I nearly broke my leg when I slipped on the custard that other fool spilled everywhere, and now you've ruined my new suede loafers. Look at them! You might as well have poured glue all over the floor!"

"I'll clear it up right away," Tom said.

"Mind you do it properly!" Bernard replied furiously. "Now, I'm going out for a walk, and if there is even the tiniest bit of stickiness on the floor when I get back, you're out of a job."

"Would you mind buying some more golden syrup?" Tom asked tentatively.

"Very well, but I'll deduct the cost

from your wages!" Bernard snapped, and he stormed off to change his shoes.

Bernard stomped out into the street. Otto had decided to come too and sauntered behind him.

"Talk about life giving me lemons!" Bernard fumed. How could he find the positive, or indeed any inspiration, in a load of gluey syrup that made his shoes stick to everything? But then he stopped, still as a statue, as an idea hit him like a thunderbolt. Sticky syrup on the floor . . . sticky syrup on the road . . . slippery custard too . . . his brain whirred away. A large grin spread over Bernard's face. "Otto, I do believe I've made myself some delicious lemonade!"

He scooted over to the supermarket,

collected a shopping cart, and filled it
with several giant tins of golden syrup
and custard. Then, Bernard found himself
walking past the cleaning products aisle. *I'll
just see if they have any suede cleaner for my
shoes,* he thought. But he couldn't see any,
so he asked a man stacking shelves.

"We don't sell it, I'm afraid, but Harry's
Hardware will definitely have some. It's just
around the corner."

"I know where it is!" He paid and then
walked with Otto over to Harry's.

Harry was just finishing helping Freddie
repair his bicycle tire when Bernard walked in.

"Hi, Bernard," Freddie greeted him.

Otto and Flapjack, who were old
enemies, glared at each other, and
Otto gave a menacing hiss.

"Hello," Bernard answered. Then seeing what Freddie was doing, he said, "Oh dear, a puncture, how unlucky."

"Yes, someone spilled several tacks outside the shop, and some got stuck in my front tire," Freddie explained.

"Really?" Bernard replied, his face lighting up.

Tacks on the road! Never mind giving him lemons, Bernard felt life was positively pelting him with inspiration. "How unlucky for you," he added, and then he turned to Harry. "Do you sell suede cleaner?" he asked.

"Yes, of course, I'll just fetch it for you." Harry returned a moment later with a small bottle. "That'll be three pounds."

"Three pounds!" Bernard exclaimed. "That's outrageously expensive."

Harry gave him a thin smile. "Would you like it, Bernard?"

"Very well, I'll take it. And I've just remembered that I need some tacks too. Let's say twenty boxes of them," he added with a smile.

CHAPTER FIVE

Bernard went home and immediately sat down at his desk. His brain was buzzing with ideas for cheating. He must have a look at his bicycle—perhaps something could be done to make that faster. He would have a chat with his friend Dodgy Dave. *Now, what else could I do?* he wondered. Bernard was thinking so hard that he barely noticed when it began to rain.

It poured all night and all the next day. Raindrops slammed angrily down on Belville, making the streets wet and slippery

and churning the surface of the canals.
But there were still four days until the
race, so everyone was pretty relaxed.

"This rain is just what we need after the
long, hot summer," Jojo said to Amira
when she came into the bakery to buy
some caramel doughnuts.

"You're probably right, but I do hope it
doesn't affect the race on Saturday," Amira
replied, looking out at the sodden street.

"It's sure to stop in a day or two," Jojo
said. "It's September after all, not February."

But the rain didn't stop, and by Friday
everyone was scanning the weather
forecast anxiously. Belville Radio began
hourly updates. The experts said it should

clear on Saturday morning, but would the roads be dry in time for the start of the race?

Friday afternoon was quiet at the bakery, so Sophie finished the tridem's decorations and their costumes, hoping that the race would go ahead. She and Amira had decided on a flower theme, so they had made masses of multicolored paper flowers. They had sewn them onto jumpsuits and hats for the three of them to wear, and stuck flowers all over the tridem. They couldn't wait to show Freddie!

Freddie and Flapjack sat in the shop with Amira and the handful of customers who had come in to escape the torrential rain. Freddie still hadn't settled on a design for the prize cake, so he was sitting with his notebook, playing around with a few ideas.

"Poor Noah," Freddie said to Amira. "I need to come up with something fantastic so that if the race doesn't happen at least he has a great cake to cheer himself up."

"The most spectacular cake you've made recently was that sailing-themed wedding cake," Amira said.

"Noah liked that too," Freddie said.

"Why don't you make a similar cake but with a cycling theme?" Amira suggested.

Freddie thought for a moment and then said, "You're so clever, Amira. That's exactly what I'm going to do!" And he began to sketch.

"Oooh, can I see?" Amira asked a few minutes later.

Freddie held up his notebook for her.

"So, it's tiered like the wedding cake.

But I'm going to create a racetrack going all the way down the cake, and then put some views of Belville on the sides of the cake using fondant icing and edible paint."

"Fantastic!" Amira cried. "And what flavor are you going to make it?"

"Well, as I don't know who's going to win it and what sort of cake they like,

I thought I'd better make each of the three tiers different, so hopefully the winner will like at least one of them."

"That's a great idea," Amira said.

"They need to be quite dense cakes for the icing to work," Freddie went on. "I haven't worked out all the details, but I thought the top could be **LEMON**, then the middle **CHOCOLATE**, maybe with some **SALTED CARAMEL** running through it, and a **RASPBERRY RIPPLE AND VANILLA** cake might be nice for the base. What do you think?"

"I think yum to all of it," Amira said, her mouth watering. "Since it's so quiet, do you want to go and get started?"

"I think I'd better—it's going to be quite a lot of work," Freddie replied, but with a smile as there was nothing he liked better than baking. He disappeared into the kitchen, Flapjack scampering along behind him.

Freddie started by baking the individual cakes. Once they were all in the oven, filling the kitchen with delicious smells, he worked on his sketch some more, adding details and deciding what colors to use where. When he was happy with it, he mixed up a large batch of **FONDANT ICING** and then divided it up to make all the different colors he would need for the cake. By that time, the cakes were baked, and while they cooled, Freddie made the figures and other objects that would be used as decorations. He decided to start with the trickiest bits, which were the **CYCLISTS**.

Once he was pleased with them, he made the **CHERRY TREES**,

the **CANAL BRIDGE**, and the **THEATRE**.

Then he sandwiched the cakes together with **VANILLA BUTTERCREAM**, cut out the racetrack, and started on the background **ICING**. When that was done, he carefully applied all the **FONDANT** figures he had made.

It was difficult and delicate work, but when it was finally finished, Freddie stood back and looked at it happily.

"Well, I'm really pleased with that," he said to himself. The cake looked amazing.

Freddie had been so absorbed in making
the cake that he hardly noticed the time

flying. He couldn't believe it when he looked at the kitchen clock and it was almost bedtime.

"I'm sorry," he said to Flapjack, who had been sitting patiently in the corner of the kitchen, waiting for Freddie to finish and take him out for a walk.

"Come on, boy," Freddie said, grabbing the lead, and together they went out for a quick wet walk in the rain. It was time to go to sleep when they got back.

I do hope the rain clears for the morning, Freddie thought as he drew his curtains and got into bed.

CHAPTER
SIX

You'll be very relieved to hear that Belville woke up to glorious blue skies and bright autumn sunshine. The racetrack was dry, and the race would go ahead!

Freddie and Amira had intended to shut the bakery at about half past ten in the morning so that Freddie had plenty of time to do the deliveries and Amira and Sophie wouldn't be in a rush getting ready for the race. But the bakery was so busy that it was a quarter past eleven before they managed to shut the door and turn the OPEN sign to CLOSED.

"I'd better scoot," Freddie said to the others, packing up the deliveries and loading them onto his bike. He lifted Flapjack into the basket and said, "I'll meet you at the start at a quarter past twelve."

"Sure," Amira said. "We'll take the cake over there for you."

"Thanks," Freddie said. "And please will you bring my costume too?"

"Absolutely," Amira said. "Don't be late!" she called to Freddie as he cycled off.

Meanwhile, over at Macaroon's Patisserie, Bernard had had a busy morning too. As soon as he'd seen that the rain had cleared, he leapt out of bed and began to get ready for the race. He was feeling very organized—his king costume had arrived from Tippy Top Tailors the day before. Bernard was **delighted** with it—he'd had a lovely time strutting about in front of the mirror, imagining everyone clapping for him as he won both the race and the best costume award.

Dodgy Dave had also delivered his bike, complete with "special features" hidden behind a shiny gold casing.

But before he could get dressed up, Bernard had work to do, sorting out his "helping hands." He didn't want to use his bike before the race, so he loaded up an old delivery cart with all his tins of syrup and custard and the boxes of tacks. He threw a blanket over the top to hide them. Knowing that Noah and his helpers would be setting up the race early that morning, Bernard waited until about half past ten and then headed off.

Right, it's eleven thirty, Freddie thought as he cycled off. *I've got 45 minutes to make all my deliveries, which should be enough time as long as nothing goes wrong.*

His first stop was Mrs. Mackenzie. She was a good friend of Freddie's and ran Belville's dog shelter, where Flapjack had come from. It was her birthday that day, so Freddie had made her a cake as a surprise. The shelter was only a few streets away from the bakery, on Blossom Lane. Freddie's journey there followed the race route, so there were big orange arrows everywhere, which would show cyclists the way.

As Freddie turned into Blossom Lane, his bike suddenly skidded **violently** across the road. He only just put his feet down in time to stop himself from falling over, and when he did, he felt like he'd stepped in glue.

"What on earth?" Freddie cried as his nose was hit by a sugary vanilla smell. He looked down to see that the road was covered in two huge puddles, one of bright-yellow liquid, and the other pale and thickly sticky.

Can it be . . . ? he wondered. He bent down and very hesitantly dipped his finger into the yellow liquid and tasted a tiny bit. "Custard," he said to Flapjack. "How peculiar! And what's this? Honey?" He tasted it. "No, golden syrup," he said.

"Are you all right there, Freddie?" a voice said behind him. He turned around to see Mrs. Mackenzie coming out from the dog shelter.

"I'm fine, but someone has spilled custard and golden syrup all over the road, which is a disaster for the race," Freddie replied.

"That's extraordinary!" she said. "Who would do such a thing?"

"Who knows? Perhaps it was an accident. But I'd better clear it up. Do you have a mop and bucket?"

"I have two mops and several buckets, so I'll help too," Mrs. Mackenzie replied. "Oh, and look, you've got another helper," she laughed and pointed at Flapjack.

Flapjack was, like
most dogs, ruled by
his stomach, and a
sea of delicious, sweet
stuff was more than he
could ignore, even though
he knew he might get told off. So, while
Freddie and Mrs. Mackenzie were talking,
he had jumped down from his basket and
begun to lick up as much custard and
syrup as he could before he was spotted.

"Oh, Flapjack, honestly!" Freddie cried when he saw him. He was about to tell him to stop, when he heard a yapping noise behind him. The dogs from the shelter had been drawn by the delicious smell too.

They **bounded** out into the road and began furiously licking up the custard and syrup, unable to believe their luck.

"Oh dear, I must have left the gate open!" Mrs. Mackenzie cried. "Quick, Freddie, let's round them up."

It must have looked like quite a sight as they herded the big group of dogs off the road and back into the shelter.

"Well, at least the road's clear now," Freddie laughed.

But then he looked at his watch. It was already a quarter to twelve! How did that happen?

"I must fly," he said to Mrs. Mackenize. "But happy birthday!" And he handed her the box.

"Oh, thank you, Freddie," she said, beaming. She opened it. "Coffee and walnut cake! How delicious! Now, you must get off so you're not late for the race."

"I must," he agreed, grabbing Flapjack.

"Good luck and thank you again!" Mrs. Mackenzie called as he sped away.

Freddie raced off to his next delivery, but when he came to Main Canal he found the arrow signs for the race were pointing straight on, toward Green Canal.

"That can't be right," Freddie said to Flapjack. "Noah said he'd changed the route away from there." He glanced at his watch. "It's five to twelve already! Where's the time going?" He sighed. "But I'll have to change the arrows—it's dangerous otherwise. Wait in the basket, Flapjack." Freddie quickly parked his bike and turned the arrows around the right way.

Back on his bike, Freddie cycled furiously down to Water Lane. He practically (but politely) threw Mr. Perkins' raspberry gateau at him and then sped along to his next stop at the museum. The streets were now crowded with people heading to the starting line in the park.

As Freddie passed the streets near Market Square, he heard the clock strike twelve fifteen. *I'm late!* he thought as he whizzed down Black Lane, rejoining the race route as it swept around toward the museum. At least that was clear of people so he could speed along. But then, just as he was about to pass Harry's House of Hardware, he saw Harry standing in the middle of the road, waving his hands in warning at him.

"Stop, Freddie!" Harry cried. "Someone has spilled tacks all over again."

Freddie stopped and looked down at the road. Except for a small area on the right, it was covered in hundreds of tacks.

"I don't believe it!" Freddie cried. "It's as if someone is trying to sabotage the race. Do you need me to help you clear them up?" he asked Harry.

"No, it'll only take a minute for me to sweep them up, but be careful as you pass around them. You get off now, Freddie, or you'll miss the beginning of the race."

"Thanks!" Freddie replied, relieved, and he raced off to the starting line.

"Good luck!" Harry called after him.

CHAPTER
SEVEN

Freddie and Flapjack reached the starting line with only five minutes to spare.

"Hi, Freddie, you're cutting it fine!" Noah exclaimed when he saw him.

"I know!" Freddie panted. He was about to tell him why, but then he decided he didn't want to worry Noah, so instead he asked, "Do you know where Amira and Sophie are?"

"Yup, they're just over there," Noah said, pointing at two figures completely covered in flowers.

"Don't they look fantastic?" Noah said. "And talking of fantastic, thank you so much for the cake, Freddie!"

"My pleasure," Freddie said.

Just then, Amira saw him and called him over.

"I am so sorry to be this late," he apologized.

"Don't worry," Sophie said. "But you do need to get changed this second."

She thrust a flowery jumpsuit and hat at him. While he put them on, Amira wheeled Freddie's bike off and parked it out of the way. Sophie transferred Flapjack to the basket on the front of the tridem and slipped a garland of flowers over his head. He looked slightly mystified but didn't object.

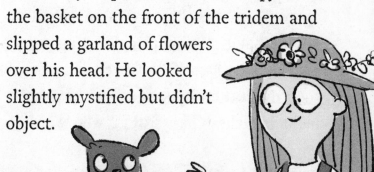

"Ready, everybody?" Noah called.

There was an excited hush as everyone got into position. Freddie jammed his flowery hat on his head and jumped on the tridem with the others.

The clock in the park chimed half past twelve and Noah shouted, "On your marks, get set, go!"

And they were off!

You won't be surprised to hear that as soon as he'd arrived, Bernard had pushed his way to the very front of the competitors, so he was one of the first away. He was feeling extra confident having spent the morning setting up his "helping hands." However, he was soon overtaken by several other people, including the Khan sisters, who were dressed as witches and riding a tandem.

Freddie and the others started off near the back of the race, but they weren't concerned. They had agreed that they would begin slowly and then, about halfway through the race, speed up. So, they took it easy and Freddie, who was at the back of the tridem, had plenty of time to look around at all the amazing costumes.

He spied Dr. Wells dressed as a
cowboy, Clarabelle Cooper, the florist,
in an amazing green-and-blue mermaid
costume, and Mrs. Desai, from the
grocer's, dressed as a Victorian lady,
riding a penny-farthing, which is a
funny-looking bicycle that looks like this:

But what really caught Freddie's
eye was the team from Macaroon's

68

Patisserie, who looked **incredible**, all
dressed in matching puffy macaron
costumes in pastel colors, riding
unicycles. They were laughing and
joking around, making everyone smile.

"Freddie!" a voice called, and he saw Jojo, dressed as an astronaut, with her bicycle decorated like a rocket.

"You look fantastic!" Freddie called to her.

"Thanks! So do you!" Jojo called back.

Up ahead, the front-runners were nearing the turn into Blossom Lane, where Freddie had found the custard and syrup. Bernard was still near the front, but as he came to the bend, he slowed right down so that he didn't slip into the sticky trap he'd left on the road. He would hang back and avoid hitting everyone else as they all fell headlong. Grinning to himself, he listened for yelps and crashes as the cyclists ahead turned the corner, but there were none. Quickly, he sped up to see what on earth was going on. He **BARGED** Mrs. Desai out of the way, sending her **FLYING**, as he pedaled around the corner, hoping to see **CHAOS**. But the cyclists were racing ahead of him, and the custard and syrup were gone.

Bernard felt a rush of **anger** and **annoyance**. Who on earth had cleared it up? Mrs. Mackenzie was standing outside her house, cheering everyone on. *I bet it was her!* Bernard thought. *Meddling old busybody!* He could feel his mood **PLUMMETING**. But then one of Drusilla's pieces of advice came back to him: **Never give into negative thinking—when something goes wrong, move on, and think about something positive.** So, Bernard took a deep breath and thought about something positive, which for him was that everyone would reach Main Canal in a moment. They would see his arrows pointing the wrong way and cycle toward Green Canal instead. *And by the time they figure out their mistake,* Bernard thought, *I'll easily be in the lead!* And, sure enough, he felt much better. So much better that he pedaled faster, **ELBOWING** several people out of the way.

Meanwhile, Freddie, Amira, and Sophie were steadily working their way nearer to the front of the race. But as they came along Blossom Lane, they saw Mrs. Desai sitting by the side of the road, rubbing her arm. Her penny-farthing was on the ground beside her. They stopped the tridem and Sophie asked, "Are you all right?"

"You are sweet to stop," she replied.

"I'm fine—I've just bruised my elbow. I fell off my bike after Bernard shoved me out of the way."

"Ow! Poor you! Can we do anything?" Freddie asked.

"Yes, you can actually," she replied. "You can go and beat Bernard! Off you go!"

They all laughed, and the Freddie's Amazing Bakery team pedaled off.

CHAPTER EIGHT

Coming up to his arrows at the junction with Main Canal, Bernard felt a rush of excitement. But then he saw the front-runners turn right, away from Green Canal, and that excitement changed to fury. Someone had changed the arrows back again!

"How dare they!" he fumed.

Bernard cycled on, but his legs were getting tired and other people kept overtaking him. Although he still had the tacks to come, and another trick up his sleeve, he felt he had to do something beforehand to get ahead.

"But what?" he asked himself desperately. And then he had a brain wave. *A shortcut! That's what I need!* He thought about the race route for a moment. "I know, Otto!" he cried. "If I go down Magnolia Canal, I can cut off a huge loop and rejoin the race after Market Square."

Have a look at the map to see what he was up to.

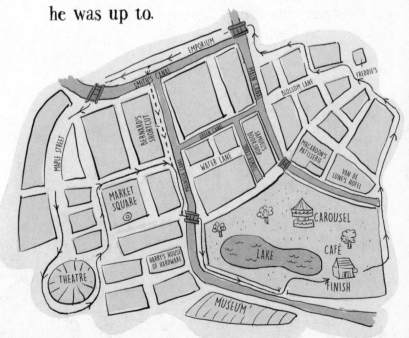

"But how am I going to avoid being seen?" Bernard wondered aloud. "I need to create a distraction so that everyone is too busy to notice me. Hmm . . . I think a bit of chaos is best." So, just as he was coming up to Magnolia Canal, Bernard deliberately **SWERVED**, causing everyone else behind him—Dr. Wells, the Macaron team on their unicycles, and Clarabelle Cooper—to all **CRASH** into each other. And then, while everyone was busy, Bernard **DARTED** down Magnolia Canal.

Freddie, Amira, and Sophie gasped as they watched everyone collide with each other ahead. Flapjack gave a bark of alarm as Sophie steered the bike over to help the racers. They parked the tridem and hopped off, helping everyone to their feet and picking up their cycles.

"That was totally Bernard's fault!" Dr. Wells exclaimed, getting back on his bike.

The Macarons made agreeing noises, and Tom pointed out, "He did the same thing last year."

"I can't believe he didn't stop," Clarabelle Cooper complained.

"Where's he gone to now?" Freddie asked, peering down Smith's Canal. He couldn't see Bernard at all.

"He must be way up ahead," Dr. Wells

said. "I'm going to try and catch him and tell him he can't behave like that." He pedaled off, followed by everyone else.

"Let's get going," Sophie said. "We can't let Bernard win."

Freddie and Amira agreed, and they picked up the pace, making their way toward the front. Freddie kept his eyes peeled for Bernard, but there was no sign of him.

That's weird, he thought. *Maybe he dropped out of the race.*

The route took them along Smith's Canal, then turned into Maple Street, swung around the theatre, and then looped back up to Market Square. Freddie, Amira, and Sophie sped up until they were in second place behind the Khan sisters.

As they rode into Market Square,

Bernard suddenly **SWERVED** out into the middle of the road, taking the lead.

"What on earth?" Freddie spluttered to Amira. "How did Bernard get there?"

"He must have taken a shortcut," she replied. "Come on. Let's try and catch him."

Up ahead, Bernard was feeling pretty pleased with himself. After scooting down Magnolia Canal, he'd had a rest and downed an energy drink before heading off to Market Square, just in front of the others. *And*, he thought with a smile, *in a minute everyone will reach the tacks that I left on the road. They're sure to do the trick.*

As he neared Harry's shop, he steered over to the right of the road to avoid

them, chortling to himself. But, as
he passed the shop, the chortling
turned to shock because, as you
know, the tacks had gone. Harry had
cleared them away before the race.

"Drat and double drat!"
Bernard yelled. Looking behind him,
he could see the Khan sisters and
Freddie's tridem, gaining on him fast.
Bernard had only one last trick up
his sleeve, and it was one he hadn't
particularly wanted to use because it
was so easily spotted. But the desire in
him to win was too strong. It was all
he wanted, all he could think about …

I have to win! thought Bernard. *I just
have to!*

So, with a cry of, "Hold on, Otto!"

he leaned down and turned a small dial on the crossbar of his bicycle.

The bicycle immediately sprang forward like a racehorse. Thanks to Dodgy Dave's handiwork, hidden beneath the gold case were wires and a battery—Bernard's pedal bike was now an electric bike.

Bernard surged back into the lead, pedaling furiously to try and cover up his cheating.

That's better! he thought as he flew through the park gates, heading toward the lake and the finish line by the café.

"How did Bernard just do that?" Sophie spluttered. "We were right behind him."

"I think someone needs to take a close look at his bicycle," Amira replied. "Come on! We can't let him win."

They pedaled as fast as they could, and they flew into the park. The Khan sisters were now a whisker behind them, but they had sped up too, so that when Bernard looked behind him, he saw everyone gaining on him.

I need to go faster! he thought frantically, and turned the dial on his bicycle up to maximum. The bike **WHIZZED AHEAD** like a motorbike. "Excellent! I'm going to finish in style!" he crowed to himself, looking at the café and finish line ahead. Noah was there, along with a large crowd of people waving and cheering, and Bernard felt himself glow with pleasure. His dream was about to come true!

CHAPTER NINE

However, right before the café, there was a bend in the road by the boating lake. Now, it wasn't a particularly sharp bend, and if Bernard had been on a normal bicycle it would have been fine. But because his electrified bicycle was going so fast, he couldn't help but lose control of it on the corner.

"Aaargh!" Bernard yelled.

And Otto let out a loud "Miahhhh!" as the bicycle, with them on it, veered off the track and careered like a galloping, runaway horse into the lake.

They both hit the water with an almighty **SPLOSH**. Bernard's crown went flying, nearly hitting a gaggle of ducks who quacked off noisily.

The crowd gasped. Noah ran over as the Khan sisters and Freddie, Sophie, and Amira cycled up. Freddie jumped off the bike.

Bernard was spluttering and splashing in the water, shouting, "I can't swim!"

"It's only a few feet deep," Noah said. "Put your feet down, Bernard, and you'll be fine."

"I can hardly stand! I feel so cold and weak. I think I'm in shock! And where's poor Otto?" Bernard wailed.

As you probably know, many cats are naturally good swimmers if they have to be, but Otto was struggling a little, weighed down by his crown and glittery cape.

Noah and Freddie sighed and exchanged glances.

"We'd better go in," Freddie said, pulling off his hat and flowery jumpsuit.

"I'll get Otto, and you help Bernard," Noah suggested, taking off his shoes.

"Are you sure?" Freddie said. "Otto can be pretty vicious."

"I know," Noah replied grimly as they both hopped in the lake. Flapjack watched this with some surprise, and then jumped in too.

Meanwhile Dr. Wells, Clarabelle Cooper, and the others were all drawing close, so Freddie turned to Amira, Sophie, and the Khan sisters and said, "I think you should finish the race before the others catch up, don't you?"

"I do," Amira replied. "We don't

want Bernard to spoil everything." And they jumped on their bikes and cycled off toward the finish line.

Freddie quickly reached Bernard, who was still making a huge fuss. Flapjack swam over and rescued Bernard's crown.

"Relax, Bernard! Come on. Let me help you to the bank," Freddie instructed, and seconds later they were hauling themselves onto dry land. Flapjack sprang up behind and presented Bernard with his crown. Bernard ignored him and then shrieked when Flapjack shook himself, showering him with water.

"I'll just get your bike," Freddie said, wading back in.

Meanwhile, Noah was trying to deal with Otto, who was every bit as mad as a wet cat can be. Noah decided it was best to just take hold of the edge of the cat's costume and gently pull him to the shore.

"Oh, poor Otto!" Bernard exclaimed as Noah delivered the furious, dripping, hissing lump of fur to him.

There was a loud cheer as someone won the race.

"Robbed again!" Bernard said bitterly, just as Freddie showed Noah the hidden electrics on Bernard's bike.

"Even if you had won," Noah said, "you would have been disqualified for cheating. Electric bicycles are not allowed."

"You don't know how hard I've worked. All the planning, the dashing around Belville this morning," Bernard said. "It's just not fair!"

Freddie and Noah looked at each other, neither of them knowing what to say to Bernard, who was being so ridiculous.

"I think I should win best costume

prize as compensation," Bernard announced. "It's only fair."

Noah's patience with Bernard had run out. "Bernard, you're unbelievable!" he said. Then Noah turned back to Freddie, who was putting his costume back on.

Once he was dressed, Noah, Freddie, and Flapjack walked off, leaving Bernard and Otto still sitting, dripping, on the bank.

Now you might expect Bernard to be grumpy and sulky after Noah said that. But he wasn't because, you see, Bernard had a bit of water in his ear. So, when Noah said, "Bernard, you're unbelievable!" Bernard thought he said, "Bernard, you look unbelievable!" So, Bernard was sitting there grinning like a Cheshire cat.

"All is not lost, Otto!" he exclaimed.
"We are still going to win the best
costume prize! Noah practically said so!"

Lots of people were still finishing, and
the crowd was cheering them on at the
finish line. Freddie and Noah found
Amira and Sophie by the café, standing
with the Khan sisters. They were all
beaming.

"Are Bernard and Otto OK?" Sophie
asked.

"Absolutely fine," Freddie replied.
"Much more importantly, who won?"

"It was a tie between us and Amira
and Sophie," Lily Khan replied.

"Congratulations, everyone!" Freddie
cried.

But Noah was looking worried.

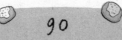

"I only have one prize," he said.

"I know, and it's not a problem," Lola Khan said. "We just wanted to compete for fun. One bike is no use to us! We love our tandem. So, Sophie and Amira are very welcome to the prize," she said.

"That's so kind of you," Amira said. "And as Sophie had her bike stolen recently, I am obviously very happy for her to have it."

"Thank you very much, all of you!" Sophie said, grinning from ear to ear.

"Well, I'm glad you all sorted that out, not me," Noah said. "I'll present it to you, Sophie, when I award the best costume prize."

"Who's going to win that?" Freddie asked.

"You'll have to wait and see," Noah

said mysteriously. He shivered slightly. "Freddie, shall we go and find some towels and a hot cup of tea, while the stragglers finish? You deserve some dog biscuits too, Flapjack."

"Yes, please," Freddie replied, and Flapjack wagged his tail.

CHAPTER
TEN

Half an hour or so later, all the competitors had finished, and it was time to present the prizes. Outside the café, by the lake, was a raised area, which was usually covered with tables and chairs, but Noah had cleared it to use as a stage. He stood there and a crowd gathered around, excited to hear the results.

"Thank you so much to everyone who took part in the race," Noah began. "I am delighted to announce that we have raised even more money than last year for the charity I set up in memory of my mom!"

There were huge cheers from the crowd.

"It's time to announce the winners," Noah went on, "starting with the race itself. It was a dead heat at the finish line between the team from Freddie's Amazing Bakery and the Khan sisters, so we have five winners. Please can you all come up here?"

Freddie and the others all went to stand at the front of the stage.

"The prize is this magnificent bike," Noah said, pointing to the gleaming roadster that was propped up at the side of the stage. "And thanks again to Ralph from Speedy Bikes for donating it."

There was more cheering.

"Now, I obviously can't split the bicycle five ways, but as poor Sophie had her bike

stolen a couple of weeks ago, everyone has
kindly agreed that she should have it."

Everyone whooped and applauded.
Sophie blushed and thanked everyone.

"And then I would also like to present the winners with some fizzy lemonade! But don't open it yet." Noah handed out bottles. "I still have to announce the winner of the best costume award."

Everyone fell silent.

"I want to start by saying what a difficult decision this has been because the standard has been absolutely fantastic this year!"

Bernard began pushing his way to the front of the crowd so that he could get up on the stage easily when Noah announced his name.

"But the winner, or should I say winners . . ." Noah said.

"That's us, Otto," Bernard muttered. "Winners!"

"They really impressed me," Noah went on, "with their original and witty costume design. So, without further ado, the winners, from Macaroon's Patisserie, are . . ."

And at that, Bernard, grinning widely, stepped firmly onto the stage with Otto following him.

Noah looked surprised. "No, Bernard, not you. It's Tom and his friends—the Macarons!"

There was a deafening cheer as the Macarons all gasped and hugged each other before running up on the stage.

Bernard, on the other hand, went crimson with embarrassment and rage.

"What?!" he cried furiously at Noah. "You said I was the winner!"

Noah looked bewildered. "No, I didn't, Bernard."

"You did! By the lake! You said I looked unbelievable and that I should win!"

"I said you *were* unbelievable," Noah replied. "Because you cheated your way around the race and still thought you should win!"

Bernard turned even redder, and there was an awkward silence as everyone turned and looked disapprovingly at him. It was like an awful version of his fantasy.

"Please could you leave the stage now, Bernard? The winners need to be presented with their prize," Noah said, and he turned away from Bernard to Freddie.

"As you all know, Freddie baked this amazing cake for the winners. Freddie, please will you present it to the Macarons?"

"I'd love to," Freddie said, carefully picking up the cake. "But I think it's a bit of a letdown for a bunch of bakers to win a cake!"

"Not at all—we're always delighted to eat one of your delicious cakes!" Tom said, and everyone laughed. Everyone, that is, except Bernard.

A red-hot FURY seized him, and, rather than leaving the stage, he LUNGED for Freddie and the cake and tried to knock it to the floor. But Flapjack, seeing what Bernard was up to, dived in front of him, tripping him and sending him FLYING across the stage, to land flat on his face.

Everyone gasped and then fell silent as Bernard lay there, scowling at Flapjack. But then something very strange happened. A voice came into Bernard's head, saying severely, "Bernard!

This is Drusilla!" Bernard froze as the voice went on. *"Bernard, shame on you. What are you doing behaving like a spoiled child? You should have paid more attention to the sixth rule: You are a winner, even when you don't win, and you must behave with dignity. Now get up, smile, apologize for your behavior, and congratulate the winners."*

The voice was so strict that Bernard found himself springing to his feet. Everyone was looking at him, and Bernard blushed as he began, "Er . . . I'd just like to . . . er . . . say," he spluttered. "I . . . er . . . didn't mean to do that, and . . . er . . . if I did it was a mistake and wrong of me, and I would . . . er . . . like to . . . er . . . say . . . s-s—" his mouth wouldn't quite say the word. "S-s-s-sorry."

Everyone looked at him with amazement. They had never heard Bernard apologize for anything.

"Are you apologizing, Bernard?" Freddie said.

"Er . . . yes," Bernard replied.

"Wow, that's a surprise," Noah said. "But a good one," he added hurriedly.

"Well done!" Drusilla said in Bernard's head. *"But you're not done yet—you must congratulate Tom and his friends."*

Bernard groaned inwardly, but, pinning a smile to his face, he turned to Tom and the others and managed to say, "And . . . er . . . congratulations!"

"Thanks, Bernard," Tom replied, looking as mystified as the others.

"Well, I think that calls for a celebration!" Freddie cried. He opened his bottle of lemonade, showering everyone in foam.

There was a lot of laughter and cheering as more bottles were popped and glasses handed out.

"I think I should cut the cake. It's so big that there should be enough for everyone to have some," Tom said, and there was a chorus of "hurrahs" and "yums."

"Before you do," Freddie said. "I'd like to make a toast to thank Noah for organizing the race, and to you all for taking part. Cheers!"

Everyone raised their glasses.

"Cheers!"

"Now let's have a party!" Freddie cried.

And, do you know what? That's exactly what they did.

ACKNOWLEDGEMENTS

The Freddie books are definitely a team effort and so I just wanted to say a huge thank you to Alex Griffiths and Dave Shephard for their brilliant illustrations, and everyone involved at OUP for all their hard work, particularly Gillian Sore, Rob Lowe, and Kathy Webb.

Harriet Whitehorn grew up in London, where she still lives with her family. She is the author of numerous books for children, and has been nominated for several awards, including the Waterstones Children's Book Prize.

GLOSSARY

BAKE to bake food is to cook it in an oven, especially bread or cakes

BATTER a mixture of flour, eggs, and milk beaten together and used to make pancakes or baked goods

BEAT to beat a cooking mixture is to stir it quickly so that it becomes thicker

BISCUIT a hard, crunchy cookie

BOIL to boil a liquid is to heat it until it starts to bubble

BRIOCHE a light sweet bread typically in the form of a small round roll

BUTTERCREAM a soft mixture of butter and powdered sugar used as a filling or topping for a cake

CAKE sweet food made from a baked mixture of flour, eggs, fat, and sugar

CROISSANT a crescent-shaped roll made from rich pastry

DOUGH a thick mixture of flour and water used for making bread or pastry

ÉCLAIR a finger-shaped cake of pastry with a cream filling

FONDANT ICING a thick icing made from water and sugar

GATEAU a rich cream cake

GLACÉ ICING	a thin icing made with powdered sugar and water
MARZIPAN	a soft sweet paste made from almonds and sugar
MELT	to melt something solid is to make it liquid by heating it
MERINGUE	a crisp cake made from the whites of eggs mixed with sugar and baked
MIX	to mix different things is to stir or shake them together to make one thing
MIXTURE	something made of different things mixed together
MOLD	to mold something is to make it have a particular shape
PASTRY	a dough made from flour, fat, and water rolled flat and baked
PROFITEROLE	a small ball of soft, sweet pastry filled with cream and covered with chocolate sauce
ROYAL ICING	hard white icing made from powdered sugar and egg whites, typically used to decorate fancy cakes
SPONGE	a soft lightweight cake
STIR	to stir something liquid or soft is to move it around and around, especially with a spoon
TART	a tart is a pie containing fruit, jam, custard, or chocolate
WHISK	to whisk eggs or cream is to beat them until they are thick or frothy

FREDDIE'S
FUNFETTI CAKE

YOU WILL NEED AN ASSISTANT, SO MAKE SURE THAT AN ADULT HELPS YOU!

The perfect showstopping party cake!

INGREDIENTS

FOR THE SPONGE

1 c. butter
1 1/8 c. superfine sugar
4 eggs
1 7/8 c. self-rising flour
1 tsp vanilla extract
1/2 c. sprinkles

FOR THE TOPPING

1/4 c. butter, softened
1 c. powdered sugar
1/4 c. sprinkles
1 tbsp water or milk

METHOD

1 Preheat the oven to 350°. Grease two round cake pans and line with parchment paper.

2 Mix together the BUTTER, SUPERFINE SUGAR, and VANILLA EXTRACT until light and fluffy.

3 Add in one EGG and mix. Then add one quarter of the FLOUR and mix. Repeat until all the EGGS and FLOUR have been used.

4 Add in your colorful SPRINKLES and mix until you have a smooth cake batter.

5 Divide the batter between the two cake pans, then bake for 25–30 minutes.

6 Transfer to a wire rack and leave to cool.

7 Once your cake is cool, you're ready to make the topping.

8 To prepare the buttercream, put the butter and water in a bowl and then slowly sift in the POWDERED SUGAR a little bit at a time while mixing.

9 Place one of the cooled cakes onto a plate and spread half of the buttercream on top.

10 Place the second cake on top and spread the remaining buttercream over the top of that.

11 Now it's time to use up the rest of your sprinkles! Sprinkle them all over the top of your cake to finish your showstopper.

VOILA!

FREDDIE'S
STRAWBERRY CHEESECAKE

An easy no-bake cheesecake
that's totally dairy free!

INGREDIENTS

9 oz. vegan cookies*
1 c. melted vegan butter
4 tbsp strawberry jam
24 oz. vegan cream cheese
2/3 c. superfine sugar
1 tsp vanilla extract
1 c. strawberries

* There are lots of
vegan cookies to
choose from—check
the package of
your favorite cookies
at the supermarket.

METHOD

1 Grease and line a cake pan with parchment paper.

2 To make the cookie base, put all of the COOKIES into a ziplock bag. Seal it carefully and crush them up using a rolling pin.

3 Mix the crushed cookies and MELTED BUTTER and stir well.

4 Add your mixture to the cake pan and press down to create an even base layer.

5 Use a spoon to spread the JAM evenly over the layer of cookie, then put it in the fridge to chill.

6 Now it's time to make the filling. Mix together the CREAM CHEESE, VANILLA EXTRACT, and SUPERFINE SUGAR, until smooth.

7 Spread the filling over the cookie base and jam. Then leave in the fridge to set for around 4 hours.

8 When you are ready to serve the cheesecake, decorate it with the fresh STRAWBERRIES.

VOILA!

FREDDIE'S

FLAPJACK'S FAVORITE PUPCAKES

Dogs shouldn't really eat golden syrup, but that doesn't mean they can't enjoy a sweet treat every now and again. Why not try making Flapjack's favorite pupcakes?

INGREDIENTS

Nonstick baking spray

2 grated carrots

2 eggs

3 tbsp runny honey

1 c. whole wheat flour

8 oz. cream cheese
for the topping

1 Preheat your oven to 325°, and spray a mini muffin tin with NONSTICK BAKING SPRAY.

2 Beat together all the pupcake ingredients until well mixed. You can add a little water if the mixture looks too dry.

3 Place a spoonful of mixture into each muffin cup and once full, tap the tin a couple of times gently on the work surface to level out the mixture.

4 Bake for 25 minutes and then leave to cool completely before removing from the tin.

5 Whip the CREAM CHEESE until smooth and then spread a thin layer onto each pupcake.

VOILA!

BORN to BAKE.

HAPPY to HELP.

Freddie Bonbon is the most
AMAZING baker in town, so when
the Belville Cake Competition
is announced, everyone wants
Freddie to win.

Everyone, that is, except rival baker Bernard,
who will go to any lengths to make
sure Freddie's showstopper cake is a
raspberry-blowing DISASTER!

FREDDIE'S
AMAZING BAKERY

THE GREAT RASPBERRY MIX-UP

WRITTEN BY
HARRIET WHITEHORN

ILLUSTRATED BY
ALEX G. GRIFFITHS

BORN to BAKE.
HAPPY to HELP.

Freddie Bonbon is the most AMAZING baker in town, but somebody loves his cakes so much they've stolen them! Who could have done such a thing?

And when superstar cat Cookie goes missing too, it looks as though the town has a mystery on its hands . . . could Freddie's little dog, Flapjack, be the one to solve it?

FREDDIE'S
AMAZING BAKERY

THE COOKIE MYSTERY

WRITTEN BY
HARRIET WHITEHORN

ILLUSTRATED BY
ALEX G. GRIFFITHS

BORN to BAKE.
HAPPY to HELP.

Freddie Bonbon is the most AMAZING baker in town, and although life is busy, he always makes time to help his friends!

So when Amira needs a new dance partner for the Summer Talent Show, Freddie steps in. But rival Bernard is waiting in the wings with some naughty tricks up his sleeve. Watch out, Freddie!